little Miss Late

by Roger Hargreaves

Late for this.

Late for that.

Little Miss Late was late for everything!

For instance.

Do you know where she spent last Christmas?

At home.

Earlybird Cottage!

But, do you know when she spent Christmas?

January 25th!

One month late!

For example.

Do you know when she did her spring cleaning at Earlybird Cottage?

In the summer!

Three months late!

For instance.

Do you know when she went on her summer holiday last year?

In December!

Six months late!

Earlybird Cottage was just along the road from where a friend of hers lived.

Little Miss Neat.

Little Miss Neat was out for an evening stroll last October when she looked over the hedge of Earlybird Cottage.

Miss Late was in the garden.

"Hello," called out Little Miss Neat. "What are you doing?"

"I thought I'd cut the grass!" replied Miss Late.

"I think," remarked Little Miss Neat, looking at the grass, "that you should have thought about that last April!"

"Tell you what," suggested Miss Neat. "Let's go shopping together tomorrow!"

"Good idea," agreed Miss Late.

"I'll meet you in town on the corner of Main Street tomorrow afternoon," said Miss Neat.

"Two o'clock!"

"I'll be there," replied Miss Late.

The following afternoon Little Miss Neat stood on the corner of Main Street at two o'clock.

Waiting for Miss Late.

She waited.

And waited.

And waited some more.

Miss Late arrived.

"Sorry I'm a bit late," she apologised.

"Sorry?" cried Miss Neat. "A bit late? It's five o'clock and all the shops are shut!!"

"Sorry," said Miss Late.

And that's what happened, all the time!

It happened when Miss Late decided to take a job.

Her first job was in a bank.

But the trouble was, by the time she arrived for work, the bank had closed for the day.

Every day!

"Sorry," she said.

They asked her to leave.

It happened in her second job, as a waitress in a restaurant.

Mr Greedy came in for lunch.

He glanced at the menu.

"I'll have everything," he grinned.

"Twice!"

He was still waiting to be served at seven o'clock.

So he went home.

"Sorry," said Little Miss Late.

They asked her to leave.

It happened in her third job, working as a secretary for Mr Uppity.

"I'd like these letters typed before I go home," Mr Uppity said to her.
He went home at four o'clock.

In the morning!

"Sorry," said Little Miss Late.

He asked her to leave.

However, as it happened, which is often the way of things, little Miss Late managed to find herself the perfect job.

She now works for Mr Lazy!

She cooks and cleans for him.

Cleaning his house every morning.

Cooking his lunch every lunchtime.

Now.

Mr Lazy, being Mr Lazy, doesn't get up in the morning like you and I do.

He gets up in the afternoon!

And little Miss Late, being little Miss Late, is always late for work.

So she doesn't arrive for work in the morning.

She arrives in the afternoon!

And.

Mr Lazy, being Mr Lazy, doesn't have lunch at lunchtime like you and I do.

He has lunch at suppertime!

And so you see it all works very well.

Very well indeed!

Last Friday evening the telephone rang in Earlybird Cottage.

Little Miss Late had just arrived home from work.

It was Mr Silly on the telephone.

"I've been given some tickets for a dance tomorrow night," he said.

"Would you like to come?"

"Oo, yes please," said Miss Late eagerly.

"Right," replied Mr Silly.

"I'll pick you up at seven o'clock!"

Last Saturday Mr Silly walked up the path to the front door of Earlybird Cottage.

He knocked.

"Come in," called a voice from upstairs.

Mr Silly went in.

"Make yourself at home," called little Miss Late from upstairs.

"I'll be down in a minute!"

3 Great Offers for MR. MEN Fans!

MR. MEN TOKEN

1 New Mr. Men or Little Miss Library Bus Presentation Cases

A brand new stronger, roomier school bus library box, with sturdy carrying handle and stay-closed fasteners.

The full colour, wipe-clean boxes make a great home for your full collection.

They're just £5.99 inc P&P and free bookmark!

☐ MR. MEN ☐ LITTLE MISS (please tick and order overleaf)

2 Door Hangers and Posters

PLEASE STICK YOUR 50P COIN HERE

In every Mr. Men and Little Miss book like this one, you will find a special token. Collect 6 tokens and we will send you a brilliant Mr. Men or Little Miss poster and a Mr. Men or Little Miss double sided full colour bedroom door hanger of your choice. Simply tick your choice in the list and tape a 50p coin for your two items to this page.

Door Hangers (please tick)
☐ Mr. Nosey & Mr. Muddle
☐ Mr. Slow & Mr. Busy
☐ Mr. Messy & Mr. Quiet
☐ Mr. Perfect & Mr. Forgetful
☐ Little Miss Fun & Little Miss Late
☐ Little Miss Helpful & Little Miss Tidy
☐ Little Miss Busy & Little Miss Brainy
☐ Little Miss Star & Little Miss Fun

Posters (please tick)
☐ MR. MEN
☐ LITTLE MISS

3 Sixteen Beautiful Fridge Magnets – any 2 for £2.00!
inc.P&P

They're very special collector's items!
Simply tick your first and second* choices from the list below
of any 2 characters!

1st Choice
- ☐ Mr. Happy
- ☐ Mr. Lazy
- ☐ Mr. Topsy-Turvy
- ☐ Mr. Bounce
- ☐ Mr. Bump
- ☐ Mr. Small
- ☐ Mr. Snow
- ☐ Mr. Wrong
- ☐ Mr. Daydream
- ☐ Mr. Tickle
- ☐ Mr. Greedy
- ☐ Mr. Funny
- ☐ Little Miss Giggles
- ☐ Little Miss Splendid
- ☐ Little Miss Naughty
- ☐ Little Miss Sunshine

2nd Choice
- ☐ Mr. Happy
- ☐ Mr. Lazy
- ☐ Mr. Topsy-Turvy
- ☐ Mr. Bounce
- ☐ Mr. Bump
- ☐ Mr. Small
- ☐ Mr. Snow
- ☐ Mr. Wrong
- ☐ Mr. Daydream
- ☐ Mr. Tickle
- ☐ Mr. Greedy
- ☐ Mr. Funny
- ☐ Little Miss Giggles
- ☐ Little Miss Splendid
- ☐ Little Miss Naughty
- ☐ Little Miss Sunshine

*Only in case your first choice is out of stock.

TO BE COMPLETED BY AN ADULT

To apply for any of these great offers, ask an adult to complete the coupon below and send it with
the appropriate payment and tokens, if needed, to MR. MEN CLASSIC OFFER, PO BOX 715, HORSHAM RH12 5WG

☐ Please send ____ Mr. Men Library case(s) and/or ____ Little Miss Library case(s) at £5.99 each inc P&P

☐ Please send a poster and door hanger as selected overleaf. I enclose six tokens plus a 50p coin for P&P

☐ Please send me ____ pair(s) of Mr. Men/Little Miss fridge magnets, as selected above at £2.00 inc P&P

Fan's Name _____

Address _____

_____ **Postcode** _____

Date of Birth _____

Name of Parent/Guardian _____

Total amount enclosed £_____

☐ **I enclose a cheque/postal order payable to Egmont Books Limited**

☐ **Please charge my MasterCard/Visa/Amex/Switch or Delta account** (delete as appropriate)

Card Number

Expiry date ____ / ____   **Signature** _____

MR.MEN   LITTLE MISS
Mr. Men and Little Miss™& ©Mrs. Roger Hargreaves

CUT ALONG DOTTED LINE AND RETURN THIS WHOLE PAGE